A Turtle in the Sun

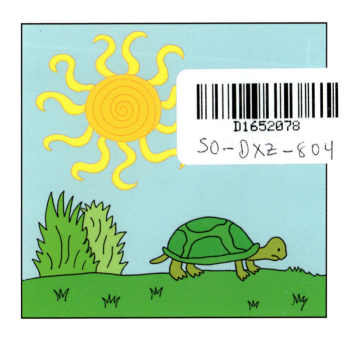

by Kris Bonnell

Here is a turtle.

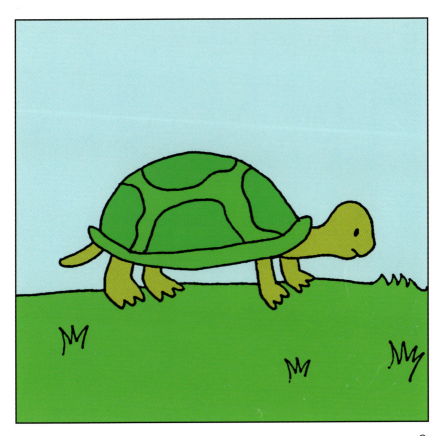

The turtle is in the sun.

He is hot.

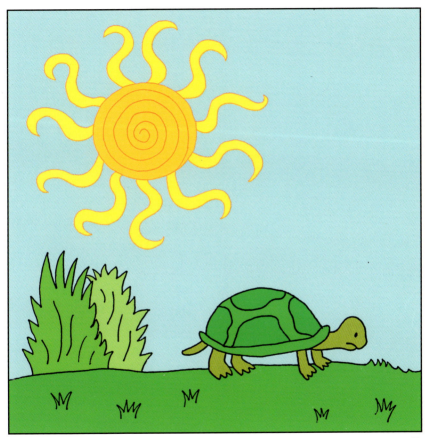

Here is a log.

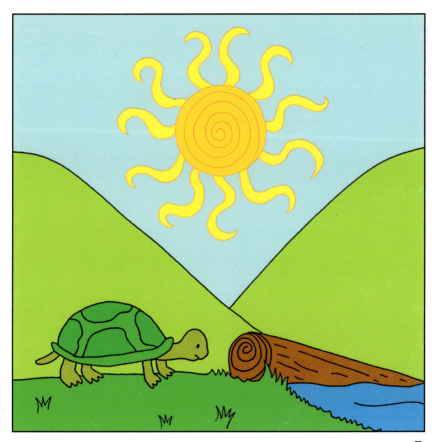

The turtle is going on the log.

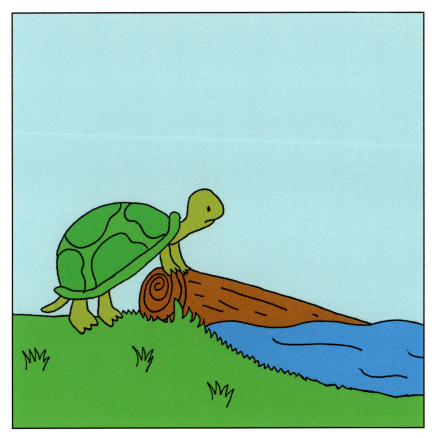

He is going
in the water.

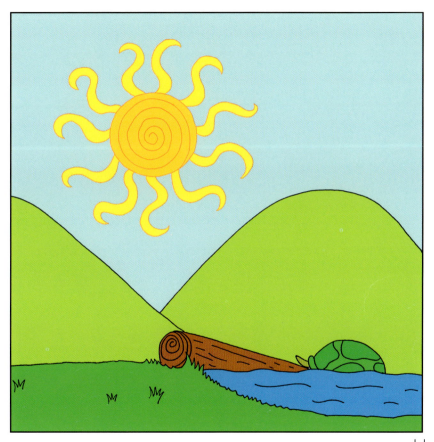

The turtle is not hot in the water!

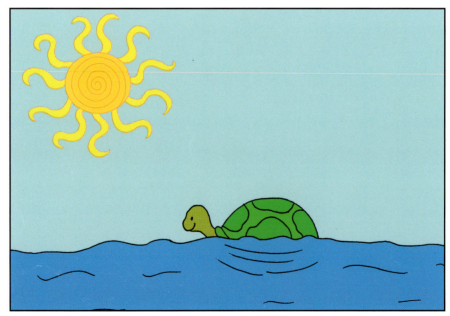